Junkyard

A Picture Tells a Thousand Dollars

NOX PRESS

books for that extra kick to give you more power

www.NoxPress.com

Also by Elise Leonard:

The **JUNKYARD DAN** series: (*Nox Press*)

1. Start of a New Dan
2. Dried Blood
3. Stolen?
4. Gun in the Back
5. Plans
6. Money for Nothing
7. Stuffed Animal
8. Poison, Anyone?
9. A Picture Tells a Thousand Dollars
10. Wrapped Up
11. Finished
12. Bloody Knife
13. Taking Names and Kicking Assets
14. Mercy

THE SMITH BROTHERS (a series): (*Nox Press*)

1. All for One
2. When in Rome
3. Get a Clue
4. The Hard Way
5. Master Plan

A LEEG OF HIS OWN (a series): (*Nox Press*)

1. Croaking Bullfrogs, Hidden Robbers
2. 20,000 LEEGS Under the C
3. Failure to Lunch
4. Hamlette

The **AL'S WORLD** series: (*Simon & Schuster*)

Book 1: Monday Morning Blitz
Book 2: Killer Lunch Lady
Book 3: Scared Stiff
Book 4: Monkey Business

Junkyard Dan

A Picture Tells a Thousand Dollars

Elise Leonard

NOX PRESS

books for that extra kick to give you more power

www.NoxPress.com

Leonard, Elise
Junkyard Dan series / A Picture Tells a Thousand Dollars
ISBN 978-1-935366-02-7

Printed in the U.S.A.
First Nox Press printing: January 2009
Second Nox Press printing: December 2009

NOX PRESS

books for that extra kick to give you more power

Marianne Williamson wrote:
"Our deepest fear is not that we are inadequate. Our deepest fear is that we are powerful beyond measure."

To my readers:

We *are* powerful.
Each and every one of us.
Including you.

I'd like to dedicate this book to one of my readers.
Daniel Noltemeyer.
Daniel is proof of how powerful one person can be.

Thank you, Daniel, for sending me those video clips
of you reading ***Dried Blood*** and ***Stolen?***.
(I ***loved*** them and thought they were really great!)

And many thanks to Dr. Melissa Rowe,
Adult Programming and Research Director,
in Louisville, KY,
for sharing the **Junkyard Dan** books with Daniel.

And I want to thank Connie Buggica for taking the
picture, and letting us use her cool car for our cover.
(Yes, I know, guys. I have a thing for yellow cars!) ☺

~Elise

Chapter 1

I was still at Violet's house.

You remember her. The old lady who used to drive the red muscle car. The car that had the vial of poison in it.

I just couldn't leave her. I felt sorry for her.

So I said I'd stay for tea.

But I'd finished my tea. And it was late.

Very late.

It had been a long day.

Not as long as Violet's, I'm sure.

But I had to go home.

I had a life to get back to.

Not much of one. But a life.

Violet? She didn't have anything to get back to.

She'd lost it all.

I felt for her.

Felt her loss. Her pain.

She looked at me and smiled weakly.

"Would you like some more tea?" she asked.

I shook my head.

"No. But thanks," I replied. "I should be headed back. It's late."

She nodded primly.

It was hard for me to have to leave her.

I'm sure it was harder for her.

We said our goodbyes.

Violet was as dignified as ever. Strong.

Like a mighty oak.

The ride back home took a lot out of me.

It was dark. And my eyes hurt.

All that crying. Crying for Violet. And Violet's daughter. And Violet's granddaughter.

I was wondering. Wondering why some peoples' lives were so hard.

Some people had it easy.

A Picture Tells a Thousand Dollars

For others? Life was hard.

I was thinking about that. Lost in thought.

Just then, my phone rang.

I took out my cell.

I saw it was Bubba.

"What now, Bubba?" I asked.

I was tired. Worn out and tired.

I just wanted to go home. Go home and go to bed.

"Where are you?" Bubba asked.

"Heading home. Why?"

"I'm over at Henry and Mel's," he said.

"That's nice," I said. I didn't know what else to say.

"Mel wants to play a game. I forget the name. You know the one. That game where you draw pictures? And guess what they're trying to draw?"

"Pictionary?" I offered.

"Yeah. That's the one. She wanted to play Family Feud. But we don't have enough people," Bubba said with a laugh.

I heard people laughing in the background.

"How many people *do* you have there?" I asked.

"Just me, Mel and Henry."

That made me laugh.

"Yes, I can see why you can't play Family Feud."

"Want to come over?" Bubba asked.

"I'm a little wiped out," I told Bubba.

"He said no," Bubba announced to Mel and Henry.

I heard a bit of a scuffle. Then Mel got on the phone.

"Oh, come on, Dan," Mel pleaded. "Please come on over."

"Even if I came over? There would not be enough people to play Family Feud." I told Mel.

She laughed.

"That's why we're going to play *Pictionary*!" she said loudly.

I had to smile.

I liked Mel.

I liked Henry, too.

Bubba could be a huge pain in my butt. But I had to admit, I liked him as well.

"Ple-e-e-e-ease," Mel said. She sounded like a little girl. Whining, but in a cute way. "Pretty please?" she added.

I smiled. It was nice having friends.

I'd never had friends like them before.

Most of my old friends were either Patti's friends. Or they were only friends because of what I could do for them.

"I'll be your best friend," she said in a sing-song manner.

I heard Henry in the background.

"Hey!" he shouted. "I thought *I* was your best friend!"

Mel giggled. "You *are*," she said to her husband. "And you always *will* be. I'm just trying to get Dan to come over."

I had to laugh.

"So, will you?" Mel asked into the phone.

I guess she was talking to me now.

Again, I smiled.

5

"You had me at 'Ple-e-e-e-ease,'" I replied.

"So you'll come over?" she asked.

"Yes. Okay," I said. "But I'm still on the road. I'll be there in about twenty minutes."

"Great!" she said.

She sounded really happy. Like it really *was* great that I was coming over.

All of a sudden? I wasn't so tired.

I wasn't so sad, either.

My spirits were lifted.

I wish I could have made Violet feel this way.

It sure felt better than being upset. And angry.

Chapter 2

They must have seen me drive up.

When I got to their front door? It swung open.

Mel, Henry and Bubba were all standing there.

"Hi," I said as I walked in.

"Yay," Mel said. "You're finally here."

I grinned. Then I threw a look at Bubba.

"Has he been driving you nuts?" I asked.

"No more than usual," Henry said.

Mel shrugged. She looked at Bubba. "Yes, he can drive you nuts. But you kind of get used to him."

Bubba cleared his throat loudly.

"Unless you haven't noticed? I *am* standing right here. I can *hear* you!" Bubba said.

He tried to look insulted.

Mel punched him on the arm.

"I *said* that we're used to you," she teased.

Bubba looked at me.

"Did you have to get used to Dan?" he asked Mel.

"No," she said. "He's normal. You? Well... you're an acquired taste."

"Yeah," Henry said. "Like snails."

Bubba made a face. "I hate snails. Who in their right mind eats snails?"

"I do," Mel said.

Bubba looked like... well, like he'd just eaten a snail.

"I ate some in France," Mel explained. "On a photo shoot. They were delicious. I didn't know what they were until *after* I'd eaten them. But they were great."

Now Bubba was happy.

"You see?" he said to me. "Mel thinks you're 'plain.' *I'm* 'delicious' and 'great.'"

Mel laughed loudly.

"No, Bubba," Mel said. "I said that Dan was 'normal.' I also said that *snails* are delicious and great. *You*, on the other hand, are just an 'acquired taste.'"

Bubba waved off Mel's comment. "Whatever," he said. "Now I know how you *really* feel about me."

He was grinning like a fool.

"I'm 'delicious' and 'great,'" he mumbled loudly.

Mel rolled her eyes, then laughed.

Henry shook his head. Then he turned to me.

"So how did things go with that vial of poison?" he asked me.

I looked at Bubba.

He shrugged. "What?!" he said. "So I talk about you a little."

A *little*?!

He tells my business to everyone! Judge Simpkins, Hilda, the sheriff, Henry, Mel, Rosa, and anyone who will listen.

"Don't you have anyone else to talk about?" I

asked Bubba.

Bubba grinned. "Not really."

"So what happened with that old lady?" Mel asked. "The one you brought to the diner?"

"Her name is Violet," Bubba said.

I nodded. "Yes, and her story is quite sad."

Mel and Henry waited quietly.

I didn't feel like going into the whole thing. It was too depressing.

"The vial of poison was from her husband," I stated.

I could see the question in their eyes.

"He was a scientist. The poison was arsenic. It was bled from pressure-treated wood. It's a long story. But he was studying a boy with autism, and looking into the boy's back patio," I explained.

Mel nodded.

"I think I get it. He thought the arsenic in the wood made the boy autistic?" she asked me.

Chapter 3

"He was working on that," I said. "But then he died of a heart attack. His work went unfinished."

"So how did the poison end up in the car?" Henry asked.

"That's the million-dollar question," I said.

"Did Violet know about it?" Bubba asked.

"No," I answered.

"So who put the poison in the car?" Mel asked.

I winced.

"You know something," Mel said.

"Yeah," Bubba said. "Spill it."

I took a deep breath. "Okay," I said. "Here's what we think happened."

I let my breath out slowly.

"Violet's daughter died of lung cancer," I said softly.

"Did she smoke?" Henry asked me.

"No. But her husband did," I replied.

Mel shook her head.

"Second-hand smoke. That's worse than smoking," she said. "There are no filters in second-hand smoke."

I nodded.

"Yes, well, her death was long and hard," I said. "And her daughter saw the whole thing."

"That must have been awful," Bubba said quietly.

I nodded. "Violet said it was. She said that her granddaughter was devastated."

"Why wouldn't she be?" Mel asked. "She saw her mother die. A slow, painful death."

I went on. "Yes, well, it turns out? The girl stayed with her father for a while. Until the selfish jerk left her. Alone. For days."

"What happened then?" Mel asked.

"Violet came and got her. The girl then lived

with Violet," I said.

"That's good," Mel said.

I nodded. "But then the girl got sick," I explained. "She was coughing a lot."

"Cancer?" Henry asked softly.

"The girl must have thought so," I said.

"She must have freaked out," Bubba said.

"And thought of her mother," Mel added.

I nodded. "We think that's what happened."

"That's *not* what happened?" Henry asked.

I shook my head. "No."

"What happened?" he asked.

"She had bronchitis."

Mel gasped.

"Bronchitis?!" Henry said. "That's not bad. Many people get bronchitis."

I nodded. "Yes. But *she* thought it was cancer."

"Did she..." Mel started to say.

Bubba turned pale.

He finished Mel's sentence. "...kill herself?"

"With that arsenic?" Henry asked.

They were waiting for me to answer them.

My eyes welled up again.

I thought of the young girl. The *confused* young girl.

"We think that's what happened," I whispered.

I tried not to cry.

"If the girl committed suicide? Her father didn't *kill* her. But he might as well have," Mel said.

"I know," I said.

I felt the need to confess.

"I cried for Violet. And her daughter and granddaughter."

Henry shrugged his massive shoulders. "So?"

"Real men cry all the time," Mel said.

"I cried when mullets went out of style," Bubba said.

We ignored him.

"Henry cried when Barack Obama got elected," Mel said. "On election night? Henry was crying like a baby."

She was looking at her husband with love.

"Hey," Henry said. "A black man was elected

president! That was amazing to witness."

"Henry. A big, black biker dude like *you* shouldn't be crying, ya big baby!" Bubba teased.

"If you knew what African Americans had to go through to get to that point, you'd cry too, Bubba."

Bubba got serious. "I know, Henry. I agree. I was only playing with you."

Henry shrugged. His eyes welled up with tears. "It's just really cool. You know, that a black man can *truly* become anything."

Mel leaned over and kissed her husband's big bald head.

That did it for the man. A tear flowed freely down his cheek.

"When we have children," Henry said to his wife. "I can now honestly tell my daughters and sons that they can become *anything* they want to become. All they have to do is work hard."

Mel reached out and wiped his tear away.

"Rosa Parks died three years too early," she whispered to her husband.

He nodded. I could tell he was really trying not to break down and let it all out.

"Boy, Dan," Bubba said to me. "You're a real party animal. The life of the party. You've got everyone crying."

Mel grabbed a pillow from the couch. She threw it at Bubba.

It hit him right smack in the face.

"Be quiet, Bubba. Henry's tears are tears of joy. Not sorrow."

Bubba picked up the pillow and threw it at Mel.

"Hey, they may be *called* throw pillows. But I don't think it's polite to *throw* them!" I offered.

"Are we going to play Pictionary? Or what?" Henry asked.

"Yes," I said. "Let's play before we kill each other."

Mel giggled. "The only one who would get killed in this group is..."

"Bubba!" we all said together.

Then we all laughed.

The serious time was over.

Chapter 4

I was finally home. In bed.

Only thing was, I couldn't sleep.

I was so tired. But I couldn't sleep.

I hate when that happens.

I was thinking of Violet.

I guess I hadn't had time to think about all that had happened.

You know, in my own mind.

To work things out. Think things through.

Violet was incredible.

Strong. Smart. Forgiving.

I hoped I had half her strength when I got to be her age.

It was with that thought that I fell asleep.

When I woke up? The sun was out.

The birds were chirping.

It was a new day.

It felt great.

A new day. A new beginning.

I got out of bed and stretched.

I looked out the window.

The dogs were starting to get up.

The cats? They were still sleeping.

It was a nice lazy day.

Sunny. Warm. Lazy. And... just what I needed.

I walked to my little kitchen.

I looked in the cupboard.

Not much there.

No cereal.

No bread.

I went to the fridge.

I had a little milk left. Not much else.

I checked the cabinet over the stove.

I had a package of Ramen noodles. And two cans of soup.

I took out a can of soup.

A Picture Tells a Thousand Dollars

I looked at it.

Chicken noodle.

I took out the other can.

Cream of mushroom.

I looked at the clock.

It was 9:07 AM.

I put back the chicken noodle.

"Today's breakfast of champions? Cream of mushroom soup," I told myself.

There were two hot dog buns in the freezer.

A couple of weeks ago? I didn't want them to get moldy. So I shoved them in the freezer.

I could put butter on them. And garlic salt.

"Mmm. Garlic bread," I added aloud.

A cat came padding into the kitchen.

"Sorry," I told him. "Not enough to share today."

I tried to crack the frozen hot dog buns open.

They broke in weird places.

Instead of having four halves? You know, from the two buns split open? I now had about 8 little pieces.

"Okay," I said aloud again. "Forget garlic bread. Now we're having garlic croutons."

Then I laughed.

If I had any more problems with the buns? I'd end up with garlic *breadcrumbs*.

A dog started barking loudly. Viciously.

I knew that bark. It was Lucky.

"Hey, Lucky," I called to the dog. "Chill out."

Lucky kept barking.

"Dan," Bubba called out. "What is *with* this dog?!"

I walked to the door and opened it. I pushed open the screen door, and let Bubba in.

"He's a good judge of character," I replied.

"Very funny."

Then I let Lucky in.

He snarled a little at Bubba. Then walked past us.

Bubba walked to the kitchen after Lucky.

"Boy, Dan. That dog sure does make himself right at home. Doesn't he?!"

Bubba opened the refrigerator door.

Then he opened the freezer.

"Yes," I said. "Like someone *else* I know who makes himself right at home in my house."

"You don't have anything good to eat," Bubba said.

Guess my comment was lost on Bubba.

"I could eat some cream of mushroom soup," he said.

"You *could*," I answered. "But you're not going to."

Bubba made a face. "Well that's rude."

Yeah. Right. *He* was calling *me* rude.

"There's only enough for one," I said.

Bubba shook his head. "You should have planned better, Dan."

"I planned perfectly well," I told him. "Breakfast for *one*."

Bubba still didn't get the hint.

He saw the bun chunks in the toaster oven. "Oh. Toast," he said. "Good. I can have some of that."

"It's not toast," I told him. "They're going to be

croutons. Garlic croutons."

Bubba's eyes lit up.

"To go in my soup," I told him. "My soup for *one*."

"Has anyone ever told you that you're chintzy?" Bubba said.

"*Me* chintzy?!" I choked out. "You're like a *leech*!"

Bubba looked insulted.

"Hey. Look, Dan. If you want me to leave. Just say so!"

"I want you to leave," I said.

He shook his head.

"No you don't."

I tried to be patient. But sometimes? With Bubba? It was tough.

He really could make me so mad.

Just then my buns went up in flames.

Not, you know, my *own* buns.

My croutons.

Chapter 5

"Hilda's diner?" Bubba asked.

"Okay," I said. "Just let me feed the animals first."

Bubba started throwing the burnt bun bits in the trash.

Lucky growled. Then he caught the charred bread as it arced to the trash can.

"I bet this dog would be great with a Frisbee," Bubba said.

I watched as Bubba threw the blackened chunks into the air.

Lucky caught each one. Then he'd swallow it whole.

"I need to feed that dog more," I said aloud.

"I think he's healing," Bubba said.

I nodded. "Yes. I think so."

"He's going to be a huge brute, once he's all healed," Bubba said.

I nodded again.

"I hope he starts liking me soon," Bubba added.

I thought of what Mel said about Bubba.

Then I smiled.

"He will. After a while," I told Bubba. "You *are* an acquired taste."

Bubba grinned.

"Yeah. And like Mel *also* said. I'm great *and* delicious."

That made me chuckle.

"I don't think you want Lucky to think that, Bubba."

Bubba had to laugh. "Yeah. You're right. Why can't I keep my big mouth shut?!"

I shrugged.

"Beats me," I told him. "I've been wondering the same thing since I met you."

With that, I went outside to feed the crew.

It took about twenty minutes.

I noticed I was low on cat food.

"I need to go to the grocery store," I told Bubba.

"After the diner, though. Right?" he asked.

"Don't you ever eat?"

"Sure," he said. "But I never turn down free food."

"Who said it was free?" I asked him.

"You're not buying?" he asked.

"If I said no, would you leave me alone?" I asked him.

"Probably not. I'd just sit there and watch *you* eat."

I rolled my eyes. "Well *that* sounds pleasant."

"It wouldn't be for me," he assured me.

"I was being sarcastic," I told him.

"Oh," he said. "Does that mean you're buying?"

I sighed heavily.

"I guess it does."

Chapter 6

"Hey, Dan," Hilda called.

"Hi, Hilda," I called back.

She came out from the kitchen.

She was wiping her hands on her apron.

"I heard you solved the vial of poison case," she said.

I looked at Bubba.

"What?!" he said. "I didn't tell her."

Hilda cackled. "Nah. For once? Someone beat Bubba to the gossip."

"That's hard to do," I said dryly.

She cackled again.

"Yup," she said. "That it is. But Henry was here this morning. He wanted some pie to take to the library. For later."

We walked toward my usual booth.

She started to take out menus.

"Don't bother," I told Hilda. "I'll have a stack of your blueberry pancakes."

"Sounds good," Bubba said. "I'll have the same."

Then he laughed.

"Just give me a side order of scrambled eggs with some bacon, too, please."

Hilda nodded and started back to the kitchen.

"Oh, and a side of sausage, too. A double batch," Bubba called to her.

Hilda stopped and turned around.

She looked at me.

"Let me guess," she said. "You're paying."

I rolled my eyes and tried not to smile.

"What else is new?" I answered.

She cackled and turned toward the kitchen again.

"Hilda?" I called out.

She didn't even turn around.

"I know. You want the same thing as he's having."

I had to smile.

How'd she know that?!

She just kept walking into the kitchen.

She came back with two cups of coffee.

She threw an old, used newspaper on the table.

"Here. This should keep you two busy while I'm cooking."

I took the main section.

Bubba took the sports.

Five minutes later? We switched.

"I need to paint my office today," I told Bubba.

"I'll help you," Bubba offered.

See? Sometimes? He was a pain in the butt. But sometimes? He came through.

"Don't you have work at the garage?" I asked.

"Nah. It's slow. I can hang out with you."

"Okay," I said. "Thanks."

It would be kind of nice to have some company.

Sort of.

A Picture Tells a Thousand Dollars

I mean it *was* Bubba.

Hilda put the plates before us.

It looked like a feast.

We really were being a bit greedy.

But I didn't care.

Hilda's cooking was amazing.

We scoffed that down in about fifteen minutes.

"How about some breakfast dessert?" Bubba asked.

"Breakfast dessert?" I asked him.

"Yeah. Some pie. You know, breakfast dessert."

I thought of the big stack of blueberry pancakes we'd just had.

"Not blueberry, of course," Bubba said.

It was as if Bubba had read my mind.

"I was thinking some apple. Maybe peach."

Again, it was like Bubba had read my mind.

"Sounds like a plan," I said.

I turned toward the kitchen.

"Hilda?" I called.

She was all the way in the kitchen. In the back.

"You boys want apple or peach?" she screamed back to us.

I had to smile. How did she *know*?!

I looked at Bubba.

He shrugged.

"I'll leave it up to you. Since you're paying and all," he said.

"We'll take two of each," I shouted back to Hilda.

"*Four* pieces of pie for *each* of you?! After *that* breakfast?!" she shouted back.

"No, no," I screamed back to her. "One of each for both of us."

I looked at Bubba.

He looked bummed.

"We *can* skip lunch," I said to Bubba.

"Sounds like a plan," he said back.

"Wait," I shouted. "Make that two of each for both of us."

Hilda was already walking to the table. In her hands were two pies.

She threw the pies on the table, then shook her

head.

"Here's one apple and one peach," she said. "Eat your fill," she added.

Then she waddled back toward the kitchen.

I think I heard her mutter the word "vultures" as she walked away.

But we didn't care.

Bubba and I just grinned at each other.

Then we dug in.

We didn't even slice them.

Just ate until half was gone, then switched.

Chapter 7

First we put on a coat of primer. That took a while.

Then we waited for it to dry.

We watched some TV.

The only thing on were court TV shows.

They were all the same.

Two parties arguing about money.

We finished one show. Then watched three more shows.

By then, we could paint.

"Are you sure you want to paint it this plain color?" Bubba asked.

"What color *should* I paint it?" I asked.

Bubba smiled. "I've always liked red."

I shook my head.

"This is an office, Bubba. Not a car."

"So?" he asked.

"So, I don't want my office looking like an insane asylum."

"Insane asylums have red walls?" he asked.

I shrugged.

"I don't know, Bubba. But I don't want a red office."

"Not just red," Bubba said. "I think you should paint it red and yellow."

"It's an office, Bubba. Not a McDonald's."

"This color is boring," he said.

"It's classic. A simple off-white."

"Boring," Bubba repeated.

"Just paint. Okay?"

Bubba shrugged. "Okay, boss. Whatever you say."

I hated when he called me boss. But he liked that I hated it. So I said nothing.

About one hundred and twenty silent minutes later? I was ready to talk again.

"So tell me about that media card," I said.

I could hear Bubba's roller rolling on the paint. So I knew he was behind me.

But he didn't answer me.

I stopped painting and turned around.

"Bubba?"

"Yeah, Dan?"

"Did you hear me?" I asked.

"Yeah, I heard you."

I put my brush down.

"Bubba," I said. "So what's up with that media card? From that totaled yellow sports car."

He stopped rolling.

Then he turned around.

His face was all red.

I didn't know if it was from working.

But to tell you the truth? We weren't working all *that* hard.

So his face shouldn't be red from hard work.

"Bubba?"

His face turned darker red.

He put down the roller.

He was blushing.

Bubba was actually *blushing*!

I couldn't imagine what would make Bubba blush.

Whatever it was? It couldn't be anything *I* wanted to know about.

"It was... freaky," he said.

"Freaky?" I asked slowly.

I wanted to prolong the answer.

"*Totally* freaky," he replied.

My mind wandered.

I wondered what Bubba would find freaky.

After all, *he* was a little freaky.

You know. The piercings. The black leather spiked collar. The all black clothes thing.

At first? If you didn't know him? Bubba *is* a little freaky.

But after you get to know him? He's not freaky anymore.

Weird? Yes.

A pain in the butt? Oh yes!

Annoying? Yes. But not really "freaky."

He only *looks* freaky.

"So what do *you* think is freaky?" I asked Bubba.

Bubba laughed.

"A short, fat, *very* hairy guy in a dress."

I laughed.

"Yes," I said. "That's freaky."

Just then the office door opened.

Henry and Mel came in.

"What's freaky?" Mel asked.

"A short, fat, *very* hairy guy in a dress," Bubba said again.

Henry laughed. So did Mel.

"Yup," Henry said. "I'd say that's freaky."

"Hey," Bubba said. "Why didn't Lucky bark or growl? And let us know you were here?"

"Lucky's a teddy bear of a dog," Henry said.

"He likes us," Mel said.

Bubba made a face. "Whatever."

"So why are we talking about short, fat, very hairy guys in dresses?" Mel asked.

She was holding a paper bag. She reached into

it.

Out came a big bag of chips. Tortilla chips.

"Ew," Bubba said to Mel. "Thanks."

Mel handed Bubba the chips.

Henry was also holding a paper bag.

He reached in his bag.

Out came a jar of salsa.

"Ew," Bubba said to Henry. "Thanks."

Henry and Mel? They were a good couple. A good team.

They finished each others' sentences. They were good together. They just... blended well.

I wondered if Patti and I had blended well together. I'd always *thought* we had. But compared to Mel and Henry? We weren't quite the good couple I'd thought we were.

The fact that I'm alone? And she's off with Neil? You know, the 23-year-old roofer? That's probably the best proof that we weren't the good couple I'd thought we were.

My mind went to Rosa.

I wondered how she was doing.

"Have you heard from Rosa?" I asked Mel.

"Yes," she said quickly. "We spoke this morning. I'll tell you about it later. I want to hear about the short, fat, hairy man in the dress."

I was shocked.

"There actually *is* a short, fat, hairy man in a dress?"

Bubba grinned. "Yeah, I just *said* that."

"I thought you were just telling me something you thought was freaky."

"No, Dan. I was talking about that media card. There really *are* pictures of a short, fat, hairy guy in a dress."

I pictured it.

I made a face.

What I'd pictured *was* freaky. And kind of gross.

"What kind of dress?" Mel asked.

Bubba looked confused.

"There are different kinds of dresses?"

"Of course!" Mel said.

"Like what?" Bubba asked.

Chapter 8

Mel sighed loudly.

"Let's see. There's sun dresses," she said.

"What are those?" Bubba asked.

"Little, bright, cute dresses you wear. Like, to the beach," she explained.

"Was the guy wearing that?" Henry asked.

Bubba shook his head.

"No," he said. "I don't think anyone would wear his outfit to the beach."

"How about a business dress?" Mel asked.

"What's that?" Bubba asked.

Mel shrugged. "You know. Simple. Bold. Conservative."

"You mean boring?" Bubba asked.

Mel shook her head.

"No," she said "Not boring. For work."

"You mean ugly?" Bubba asked.

"No," Mel said. "Not ugly."

"Well, he sure did look ugly in it!" Bubba said with a snort.

Then he laughed out loud.

"I don't think it was a work dress," Bubba said.

"Was it casual?" Mel asked.

"*Casual*?!" Bubba repeated. "I have no idea what that means! In terms of a dress, that is."

I looked at Bubba. "It means 'for everyday use.'"

Everyone looked at me.

"What?!" I said. "I *was* married."

They were all smiling at me.

"It's not like *I* wore dresses!" I said loudly.

They were still smiling.

"My *wife* wore them!" I added.

Bubba waved his hand at me. "Whatever."

Then he laughed.

That's when I knew he was just busting my

chops again.

"If what Dan says is true?" Bubba said. "Then it wasn't casual."

"What about formal? Was the dress formal?" Mel asked.

"What's that mean? Dress wise," Bubba asked.

"You know," Mel said. "Like... eveningwear."

Bubba thought about that.

"Maybe," he said. "I mean, the guy? He looked *horrible* in it. But if *you* were wearing that dress..."

Bubba looked off into the distance.

He was grinning like mad.

He was picturing Mel in the dress. The dress the short, fat, hairy guy was wearing. Wearing in the pictures.

"Hey!" Henry shouted. "Bubba! That's my *wife* you're day-dreaming about!"

Bubba blinked his eyes. Then he shook his head quickly.

"Oh," Bubba said. "Sorry, Henry."

"Yeah, well, knock it off!" Henry said.

"Why are you apologizing to *him*?" Mel asked Bubba. "You should be apologizing to *me*!"

This was getting out of hand.

And totally off topic.

"Can we *please* get back to the pictures?" I asked.

Bubba nodded.

"Yeah. Sure. Well. Lets see," Bubba said. "The guy was wearing a shiny pink dress. Tight. Showed way too much!"

Bubba made a face.

"It had these little, thin straps," Bubba said.

He put his fingers between his neck and shoulders.

"Spaghetti straps?" Mel asked.

Bubba looked at Mel. "I don't know."

"Those are usually found on gowns," I told Bubba. "It's either those, or the dress is strapless."

Again, everyone looked at me.

"I was *married*, folks!" I shouted.

"Dan's right," Mel said. "So it was an evening dress."

Bubba shrugged.

"I don't know *what* it was. But his bra straps were showing."

Then Bubba laughed. Hard. A full belly laugh.

"That sounds so funny! *His* bra straps were showing."

Henry and I joined Bubba. We were all laughing like fools.

Then Mel said, "That's so tacky! Your bra straps should *never* show!"

And the funny thing was? She was *serious*!

Henry, Bubba and I laughed for about ten minutes longer.

Chapter 9

Mel made a face. "Are you guys done?"

"Sorry, babe," Henry said.

"We're not laughing at you," I told Mel.

"It's just so... weird," Bubba said.

Mel smiled.

"Show us the photos," she said.

Henry nodded.

"I want to see them, too," he said.

I shrugged.

"Me? I can live without seeing them."

Mel punched my arm.

"You know you want to see them!"

I shook my head.

"Nope."

"Not even one?" Henry said.

"Not even one," I said.

Mel turned to Bubba. "Show *us*!"

Bubba took out his wallet.

He slipped out the media card.

"You mind?" he asked me.

He was pointing to my computer.

"Help yourself," I said.

They all ran to the computer.

Bubba turned it on.

We waited for it to load up.

"Pass the tortillas, please," I said.

"Want salsa?" Henry asked.

"Sure."

I scooped up some salsa.

"Wow! This is good!" I said.

I had some more.

"What kind is it?"

I reached for the jar.

It didn't have a label.

"Mel makes it," Henry said.

"From scratch?" I asked.

Mel nodded.

"With love," she said.

She giggled.

"It's *really* great!" I said.

"It's all natural," she said.

Bubba stuffed some in his mouth.

"Who cares?!" Bubba said. "It tastes *great*!"

"The best I've ever had," I said.

"If the super-model thing doesn't work out? You can always make salsa," Bubba said.

Mel giggled again.

"In *this* economy? No way!" she said.

"Why not?" Bubba said.

"Yeah," Henry said. "Paul Newman did it. His salad dressings? His pasta sauces? They're great!"

"You can call it 'Mel's Own.'" Bubba said.

Mel giggled again.

"That sounds awful," she said. "It sounds like calzone."

"Would you people stop talking about food? I'm getting hungry," Bubba said.

Henry laughed.

He shook his head.

He looked at Bubba.

"You're *eating* chips and salsa! How can you be hungry?"

Bubba shrugged.

"I don't know. I just am."

Bubba shoved the media card in the slot.

Before I could look away?

They popped up.

The pictures.

"Oh, my God!" I shrieked.

I hadn't wanted to see them!

Just for this reason!

Now?

Now I wanted to burn my eyes out!

With a hot poker.

Chapter 10

"Oh, my God!" Mel said.

"You're not kidding!" Henry added.

Bubba squinted.

"See? I told you!" he said.

"That's..." Mel was looking for the right word.

"Hideous!" I said.

Henry nodded.

"It *really* is," he said.

There was no other word.

Those pictures? They were... hideous.

"I know," Bubba said.

Then he cried out.

We all looked at him.

"I just threw up a little. In my mouth."

"Maybe because you're eating too many chips," Mel said.

"Or maybe, because that guy is *butt ugly*!" Bubba replied.

It was hard to look at the screen.

I was repulsed.

So was Henry. I could tell.

So was Bubba.

Mel? She didn't seem to mind so much.

Henry was trying not to look.

Then, he squinted.

He stared at the computer screen. The monitor.

"Can you scroll through those?" Henry said.

Bubba laughed.

"You want to see *more*?"

Henry shot a look at Bubba.

"Just scroll through them. Can you?"

Bubba shrugged. "Sure."

Henry leaned close to the screen.

Photo after photo appeared.

"He looks like he's modeling," Mel said.

"He's one butt ugly model," Bubba said.

Henry was staring at the pictures.

He let out a loud groan.

"What's the matter, honey?" Mel asked.

"You're not going to believe this," Henry said.

"What?!" Bubba said to Henry. "You have the same dress?"

Henry ignored him.

I, on the other hand, laughed.

When Henry didn't answer? I got nervous.

It got really quiet.

Too quiet.

It was creepy.

"Please tell me you don't wear dresses," I said to Henry.

Henry was still looking at the hairy man.

Then he looked up at me.

"No," he said. "No dresses."

"I kind of like the dress," Mel offered.

Then she giggled.

"Not on the man, of course. But *I'd* wear it," she said.

"And you'd look goo-oo-ood!" Bubba said.

Henry threw Bubba a look.

"Bubba," he said. "What did I tell you about that?"

Bubba threw his hands in the air.

"Hey," Bubba shot back. "*You're* the one who married a super-model!"

Again, we were getting off topic.

"So what's up?" I asked Henry.

I nodded at the monitor.

"I'm not sure..." he started.

"Not sure? About what?" Mel asked.

"I, um, think he's a patron. Of the library."

We all went silent.

Chapter 11

Bubba shrieked.

"You mean you *know* this guy?!"

Henry grimaced.

"I think so."

"Oh, God," Mel said.

"Yeah," Henry said.

Bubba started cracking up. "How are going to *face* him?"

Henry leaned into the screen.

"Can you make the pictures larger?" he asked Bubba.

"Oh, God," I said. "Please don't!"

"I want to see if it's him."

I looked away.

A Picture Tells a Thousand Dollars

When Henry, Bubba and Mel groaned? I knew they had blown up the photos.

Henry spoke softly. "Oh, no."

"Is it him?" Bubba asked.

"Yes."

"You sure?"

"Yes."

"Positive?"

"Yes."

I looked at Henry. "So now what?"

He shrugged. "I don't know."

"Do you know his name?" Bubba asked.

Henry nodded. "Yes."

"What is it?"

"I can't tell you, Bubba. He's a *patron*. Of the *library*."

Bubba laughed.

"What?! That's 'inside' info?"

"Yes," Henry replied.

"You're not a *doctor*, Henry! Or a lawyer! You're a *librarian*."

Henry shrugged.

"It doesn't matter, Bubba. I will not tell you the name of the patron."

"You're just being a jerk," Bubba said. "It's not like you can lose your *license* or anything."

Then Bubba started laughing.

"Ha. That's funny. Get it? Like using your doctor's license? Or your law license?"

Bubba thought he was hilarious.

We didn't think so.

"You're a librarian! You work in a library!"

"So? People have rights. I honor and protect my patrons."

"Hey," Mel said. "Speaking of lawyers? Let's call Rosa. She'll know what to do."

My heart fluttered a little.

Rosa.

A reason to call Rosa.

I smiled.

"Want me to ask her?" I asked.

Mel was Rosa's friend.

I knew that.

But if Mel called Rosa? I wouldn't get to speak

with her.

Mel grinned.

"Great idea," Mel said.

She elbowed Henry in the ribs.

"Ouch. Ah. Yeah," Henry said. "*You* call Rosa."

Henry was looking at me. And rubbing his ribs.

Then he turned to his wife.

"Very subtle, dear," he told Mel.

Normally? I would have been embarrassed.

But I wasn't.

I was too excited. Excited about calling Rosa.

Having a *reason* to call Rosa.

By now? It was evening.

Rosa should be home from work.

"I'll dial," Mel said.

She rushed to my phone and dialed.

I rushed right behind her.

Mel listened. "It's ringing."

She shoved the phone at me.

"Hello?" I said into the phone.

It was still ringing.

Everyone was looking at me.

"Sorry. It's still ringing," I told them.

"She's probably not home," Bubba said.

I was thinking the same thing.

My heart sunk a little.

I was about to hang up.

Just then? I heard her voice.

"Hello?"

She sounded out of breath.

"Rosa?"

"Yes? Is this... Dan?"

I heard her sharp intake of breath.

"Yes, it's me."

"Oh. Good," she said.

I heard keys jingling.

"Is this a bad time?" I asked.

"No. I just walked in."

"Want a few minutes?"

"No. Now's good. Great, really."

"You sure?"

"I'm sure," she said sweetly.

There was a long silence.

A Picture Tells a Thousand Dollars

For me? I was thinking about Rosa.

Picturing her. In my mind.

Her smile.

Her eyes.

Her hair.

"So, um..." she said.

"So, ah..." I said.

"***Ask her***!" Bubba yelled.

My mind snapped back.

Back to reality.

Here and now.

"Ah, I have a question for you," I said.

"Yes?" she said softly. Slowly.

"Oh. Wait. Not *that* kind of question," I said.

Oh, yeah. I was smooth. Huh?

A real ladies man.

A player.

I heard Bubba mutter. "This is painful."

"Shut up, Bubba," Mel said.

"Yeah," Henry added. "Let's let the man talk."

Henry grabbed Bubba's shirt. Then dragged him from the room.

Chapter 12

"Okay they're gone," I said.

"Who's gone?" Rosa asked.

"Bubba, Mel and Henry."

"Mel's there?" Rosa asked.

"Yes."

"Lucky Mel," she said softly.

I smiled.

Rosa said the nicest things.

She made me feel happy.

Like a kid.

"Can I start over again?" I asked.

"Start what?"

"This call."

"Oh," she said. "Do you want to hang up?"

"No. I just want to start over again."

"Oh. Okay."

I smiled "Okay."

I waited a few seconds.

I had to get my head together.

I took a deep breath.

I let it out slowly.

Then I started again.

"Hello, Rosa?"

"Yes?"

"It's me. Dan."

"Oh. Hi, Dan! Great to hear from you!"

See? This was going better already.

"Did you just get home from work?" I asked.

She giggled.

She sounded so adorable.

"A couple of moments ago."

"Is this a bad time?"

She paused.

"Not at all, Dan. Any time you call will be perfect."

Okay. Now I was all twisted up inside again.

In a good way.

But still, all twisted up.

"So, to what do I owe this honor?" she asked.

Okay. I could do this.

"It's about a guy. In a dress. Henry knows him."

I heard a groan. It came from the other room.

It sounded like Bubba.

I heard the word 'painful' again.

I had to side with Bubba on this.

It really was painful.

For *all* parties involved.

"Sooo," Rosa said.

"Well, he's a patron. At the library."

"And he wears dresses?"

"Well, only one. That I know of. A shiny pink one."

Dead airspace.

"His bra straps show. Mel said that that was tacky."

"I'd have to agree," Rosa said.

More dead airspace.

"And you're telling me this because..."

"Because we don't know what to do."

"About what?"

"The media card."

"What media card?"

"The one with the pictures on it!"

"Oh. Oh. You found the card?" she asked.

"Well, Bubba did."

I heard her giggle.

"Figures," she said. "If it's something weird? Bubba's usually involved."

"Yes, well. We don't know what to do."

"About what?"

"About the media card."

"Where did Bubba find it?" Rosa asked.

"In a car. In my yard. A little yellow sports car."

"Is it the man's car?"

"I don't know."

"Can you find out?" Rosa asked.

"Yes."

"Then that's your first step."

Chapter 13

I panicked.

I said, "Okay."

Then I hung up.

The minute I hung up?

I regretted it.

But like I said. I panicked.

When you panic? Nothing good ever comes of it!

Mel, Henry and Bubba came back.

"So what did she say?" Mel asked.

"She said we need to find out who owned the car."

"What car?" Mel asked.

"The car that had the media card in it."

"Oh. Right," Mel said.

"That makes sense," Henry said.

Bubba snorted. "It would still be easier if Henry would just tell us who the guy is."

Henry shook his head. "I'd rather not."

"Look," I said. "Rosa's right. Let's try this first."

We all walked to the little yellow car.

It had been side swiped.

All along the passenger side.

The insurance company totaled it.

That's when it was brought here.

Before my time, of course.

Lucky walked with us.

He liked Mel and Henry.

He showed his teeth to Bubba.

"Why doesn't he *like* me?" Bubba whined.

"Give him time," I said.

Mel laughed. "Yeah. Then he'll *really* want to bite you!"

I got the VIN number from the car.

"You guys might as well go home," I said.

63

"Kicking us out so soon?" Mel asked.

"No. Not at all," I said. "I'll have to ask Judge Simpkins to help me out with this."

"So?" Bubba asked.

"So it's too late to ask him tonight. I'll have to call him tomorrow."

"Okay," Mel said.

"But let us know what happens," Henry said.

"Yes," Mel added. "My husband will be worried about this."

Henry shrugged. "Hey. I don't want to invade my patrons' privacy."

Mel leaned over and kissed his big bald head.

"You're a good man, Henry. That's why I love you."

Seeing them together made me think of Rosa.

I was an idiot to hang up on her.

She must think I'm a real jerk.

I'm not. You know, a jerk.

I just get so nervous around her.

Even on the phone.

That's even worse for me.

"Want me to help you finish painting?" Bubba asked.

I smiled.

I'd forgotten all about that.

"No. But thanks, Bubba. I can finish on my own."

"You sure?"

"Yes. Thanks."

"What about the clean up?" he asked.

"I can do that, too. Thanks, Bubba."

"Okay, bud," he said.

I watched as Mel, Henry and Bubba left.

They really were good friends.

I didn't mean to rush them out. But in a way, I did.

I wanted to call Rosa back.

Chapter 14

"Hello?"

"Hello, Rosa?"

"Dan?"

"Yes, it's me."

"That was fast. Did you find the owner?"

"No. I don't have that info. I have to do it tomorrow."

"Oh."

"I just wanted to call you back."

"Oh. Okay."

"So what's new?" I asked.

"I put my groceries away."

"No. Not since I last called. You know. Lately."

A Picture Tells a Thousand Dollars

"What's new *lately*?" she asked.

"Yes."

"Oh. Well. I, um..."

I could tell she was thinking.

"Not much is new, really."

I had to laugh. "Same here. Not much is new."

"I *do* miss home," she said.

That was great news. For me.

"And my dad," she added.

That was sad news. For her.

"Well, I know we miss you here."

She giggled. "Really?"

"Oh yes. Your name pops up all the time."

"Good things, I hope."

"Oh yes," I told her. "All good things."

"That's good."

"Yes," I replied.

There was a long, silent pause.

"I painted my office today," I blurted out.

She laughed.

A light tinkling sound.

"Let me guess. White?"

"No! Are you *kidding*?! How boring."

"So? What color?"

"A nice egg-shell," I replied.

"You mean, *off* white."

She laughed again.

"Yes," I said. "But it's *way* off."

"Way off what?"

"Way off *white*."

That made her laugh again.

I loved hearing her laugh.

I could listen to her laugh for the rest of my life.

Then it hit me.

I really could!

I *could* listen to her laugh... for the rest of my life.

I got nervous again.

"So when are you coming home?"

I sounded desperate.

I knew that.

I could've kicked myself.

But I had to know.

"I thought I'd come back for a visit soon."

"When?"

She paused.

"I don't know. When would be good for you?"

Without thinking? I replied.

"Tomorrow."

She laughed again.

"That would be nice," she said softly.

Intimately.

"But I'm seeing clients tomorrow."

"Oh," I said.

I was bummed out.

"So when is the soonest you *can* come?" I asked.

"I don't know," she said. "Let me check my schedule. Then I'll get back to you."

"Okay."

"When, *really*, is good for you?"

She sounded serious.

So I answered seriously.

"Rosa? *Any* time you get here would be great for me."

Chapter 15

I had to clean up the painting stuff.

But I did it with a grin on my face.

In fact? The paint had hardened on the rollers. And the brushes? Hard as rocks.

Normally? I wouldn't be too pleased about that.

But ask me if I cared.

I didn't.

My talk with Rosa?

It was perfect.

Not the first one. The second one.

The second talk? It made up for the first one.

By ten times.

A million times!

It was perfect.

So that's why I was smiling.

I even went to bed smiling.

Still thinking about our talk.

She was coming home. For a visit. Not moving back. But coming home.

It was a start.

I was *still* smiling as I fell asleep.

*   *   *

I woke up the next morning.

Still smiling.

I fed the dogs and cats.

Then I called Judge Simpkins.

He answered the phone.

"You've reached the office of Judge Simpkins. Please leave a message."

"Judge? Is that you?"

"Who's this?!" he roared.

"It's Dan. Dan Corbett."

"Oh, hi, Dan. How goes things?"

I had to laugh.

"What was up with that?"

"With what?" he asked.

"The way you answered the phone."

"Oh. My secretary is in the bathroom. I was about to make a call. The phone rang as I picked up the phone."

"And?"

"And I didn't want to answer it. I wanted to *make* a call. So I hoped the person calling would just leave a message and hang up."

I had to laugh.

"Sounded like a plan," I said.

The judge laughed.

"Not really," he said. "It didn't work. Did it?!"

"I can call back."

"No, Dan. That's okay. I don't mind speaking to *you*."

"I'm just calling for the name of an owner of a car. I have the VIN number."

"The car that had the funny pictures in it?"

I sighed. "Bubba, again?"

The judge laughed. "That boy would blabber military secrets to the enemy in no time!"

"Good thing he doesn't know any military secrets."

The judge laughed so hard, he choked.

"'Tis true, my son. 'Tis true."

I heard some papers shuffling around.

"Okay, Dan. What's that VIN number?"

I gave him the number.

He repeated it.

"Is it true that the man was wearing a little pink number?"

I shuddered with the memory.

"Yes," I said. "It's true."

The judge laughed.

"And was he as hairy as Bubba said?"

Again, I shuddered with disgust.

"Yup. He looked Italian. His back looked like brown carpet. *Shag* carpet. Like from the 70s."

The judge laughed.

"Full head of hair?" he asked.

"Thick and dark."

"Life's not fair," he said. "He has all that hair all over the place. And I'm as bald as a cue ball."

Chapter 16

"Houston, we have a problem."

"Dan? Is that you?"

I'd called Henry at the library.

"Yes, it's me."

"What kind of problem?"

"The owner of the car? Female."

"So?" Henry asked.

"If that's his wife? And she doesn't know about his..."

"Oh. Oh. Right. I get you now," Henry said.

"If I tell you the lady's last name? Would you tell me if it's the same as his?"

Henry thought about that.

"I don't know. Tell me her last name first."

"What are we? In grade school?" I asked.

"You want my help?"

"Yes."

"Then tell me the lady's last name."

I did.

Henry didn't reply.

"Henry?"

"Yes, Dan?"

"Is it the same name?"

"Well, Dan. You know what you said when you called?"

"What?"

"'Houston we have a problem.'"

"Yes?" I asked.

"Well, Houston? We *have* a problem."

"Different name?" I asked.

"Well maybe it was his daughter's car. And she's married. And has a different last name."

"Henry, would *you* give your daughter those pictures of yourself?"

"Oh. Right. I forgot about that."

I was talking aloud now.

Not really asking Henry.

Just thinking aloud.

"Why would a *woman* have those pictures?"

"I don't know, Dan. What do you think?"

"Who knows? Extortion? Blackmail? A shakedown?"

Henry gasped.

"You *think*?"

"I don't know. I can't think of any other reasons. Can you?"

"Not at the moment," he said.

We were both lost in thought.

"Now I want to help the guy," Henry said.

"What changed?" I asked.

"If he *is* getting blackmailed? That's not right."

"No, it's not."

"And I want to help him," Henry said.

"How?"

"I don't know. I've never done this before."

I thought about that.

"Look, Henry. The guy must be nice. Or you wouldn't protect him as you are. You also wouldn't want to help him."

"That's true. So what?"

"So, things might get... weird between you. If you talk to him."

"Yes," Henry said. "That's true."

"He might not come back into the library. If he gets embarrassed."

"That would be a shame. He loves to read."

"So why not let *me* talk to the guy?"

Henry thought about that.

"Only you, Dan. Not Bubba."

That made me laugh.

"Have I ever had Bubba help with any of these, ah, cases?"

"No."

"Well, I'm not going to start with this one."

"Okay, Dan. Come to the library."

I rolled my eyes.

"Henry, can't you just tell me?"

"No. I won't betray my patrons like that."

"Then how am I going to help this guy?"

"Well," Henry explained. "If you just *happened*

to be in the library? And the guy's name and contact info was up on my screen? I wouldn't be *giving* it to you."

I rolled my eyes again.

Henry had his ethics. That was a good thing.

And he *is* a good man.

So I didn't argue with him.

I mean, in the end? It was the same thing.

But he felt better about it.

So I went to the library.

Chapter 17

"You sure you will treat him with respect?"

"Of course, Henry!"

"What will you say to him?"

"I don't know. I have to see how things go. How he reacts."

"You won't tell him where you got his name from?"

"No, Henry. Don't worry. I promise. He'll never know."

Henry looked upset.

"Look. If he isn't getting blackmailed? I'll just give him the media card. But if he *is*? Don't you want to help him?"

Henry nodded. "Yes."

"So let me help the man."

Henry slapped me on the back.

"Okay, Dan. The man *might* need help."

I had to smile.

"I can't give him *all* the help he might need. But I *can* try to help him if he's getting blackmailed."

Henry nodded.

"I trust you, Dan."

"Thanks, Henry. That means a lot to me."

*　　*　　*

I drove to the guy's house.

No one was home.

I turned to leave.

"Excuse me," a woman called.

She was in the driveway next door.

"May I help you?"

"Yes," I said. "I'm looking for the owner of this house."

"He's at work," she said.

I nodded. "I figured."

"You can reach him at the zoo."

"The zoo?"

"That's where he works."

"Okay. Thanks," I said.

Then I drove to the city. To the zoo.

When I got there? I walked to the gate.

There was a girl in the booth.

"Ticket for one?" she asked.

"I don't know if I need a ticket," I said. "I just want to speak with Mr. Izzo."

"He's our president. And the CEO, too. You know, the Chief Executive Officer."

"Oh," I said. "I didn't know that."

She nodded. "I'll call his office."

"Thanks."

She nodded again.

"Wilma? There's a man here to see Mr. Izzo."

The girl looked up at me. "Why?"

"I, ah, have something of his."

She nodded. "He has something of his."

She looked up at me again.

"What?"

"It's kind of personal," I said.

"It's kind of personal," the girl repeated into the phone.

She listened.

"What is it?" the girl asked me.

"I'd rather not say."

"He'd rather not say."

She listened some more.

"Will it fit in an envelope?" she asked me.

"Yes."

"Wilma said to leave it in an envelope."

The girl started to look through her drawer.

Probably for an envelope.

"I'd rather not," I said.

"He'd rather not."

The girl listened.

She nodded.

Then she rolled her eyes.

Then she looked to see if I was watching.

I was.

"Okay, Wilma. Will do," she said.

She hung up the phone.

Chapter 18

I followed the girl's directions.

The office was on the other side of the zoo. In an office building.

Right before I got to the building? My phone rang.

It was Bubba.

"Dan? It's me. Bubba. Look. A tow truck stopped by the garage. They were bringing a car to your yard."

"Okay, Bubba. Can you let them in for me?"

"I already did."

"Thanks."

"I was looking through the car. Dang, it's a shame! It was a beauty. An old Cobra. Black. Was *mint*. Before it got wrapped around a pole. Great stick shift! It's a snake. A cobra. With *ruby* eyes!"

"I'll do the paperwork when I get back," I said. "I'll put it in the computer system, too."

"Okay, Dan. Just wanted you to know. Oh, and I found something in the car."

Oh, God. *Now* what?!

"It's a present. Wrapped up real nicely."

I took a deep breath.

"Okay. I'll handle it when I get back. *Okay*?!"

"Yeah, Dan. Cool your pits. So what are you doing?"

"It's none of your business," I said.

Then I hung up the phone.

I know. I was rude. But I was tired of all these problems.

I just wanted to be left alone. Live a simple life.

I arrived at the office building.

I went inside.

Mr. Izzo's office was on the top floor.

I went into his office.

"Are you Wilma?" I asked.

"Yes."

"I'd like to see Mr. Izzo."

"What is this in reference to?"

"It's personal."

She made a face. "So you said."

I didn't wait for her to kick me out.

I strode to the door and knocked.

A man called out.

"Come in."

The minute I saw him? I knew it was him.

He was wearing a dark suit. White shirt. Dark maroon tie. Black dress shoes.

He looked like a businessman. All work. No play.

He held out his hand.

"Guido Izzo. How may I help you, Mr., um...?"

"Corbett. Dan Corbett," I said.

His handshake was firm.

I didn't know what I was expecting. But it wasn't that.

"I own a junkyard. An auto junkyard."

"Yes?"

"And a media card was found. With some pictures."

He looked at me head on.

"Very *private* pictures," I said.

His eyes grew large and round. "Were they…?"

He didn't know how to word the question.

I didn't know how to word the answer.

"Of you," I said simply.

He swallowed hard. "Wearing…?"

I didn't let him finish his sentence.

"Yes."

His face turned white.

I took out the media card.

I handed it to him.

"Here," I said.

He took the media card.

He walked to the office door and closed it.

"Mr. Corbett. I can't thank you enough for this. It's been a long year for me."

"How so? And please, call me Dan."

He nodded.

"I was being blackmailed. Extorted."

"I suspected so."

He nodded. "I'd paid. And paid. And paid. And then it just stopped. The blackmail just stopped. But I'd never gotten the disk, as promised."

"It was in a car that was totaled. Maybe your blackmailer didn't know where the card went to in the crash? Things fly all over the place during accidents. Get themselves wedged into weird cracks. Maybe your blackmailer didn't know where the card went to."

"Maybe," he said. "But the 'not knowing' was even worse than the blackmail!"

"I can imagine," I replied.

He shook my hand again. "I owe you *big time* for this."

"You owe me nothing, Mr. Izzo. Just keep your blinds closed when you… ah… indulge."

He nodded and pumped my hand. "Will do, Dan. Will do. And please. Call me Guido. Do you have a business card? With your info? I'd like to give you a lifetime membership to the zoo."

"You don't have to do that," I said.

"I want to. I want to return the favor."

I thought of Rosa. "Okay, Guido. Thank you."

"It's the least I can do for putting my mind at ease."

I didn't know what else to say.

It was time to leave.

I gave him my card. Then headed for the door.

"Well, call me if you need anything."

Guido Izzo nodded. "I will. And the same goes for you."

I nodded. "Will do."

I hadn't expected to ever hear from him again.

But I was wrong.

When I got back to the yard? I had voicemail.

"Dan? It's Guido Izzo. You're not going to believe this. But the media card? It's been stolen."

TO BE CONTINUED

It seems Dan is not done solving this problem yet. Read the next **JUNKYARD DAN** book, entitled **WRAPPED UP,** to find out who stole that media card from Guido Izzo. Who could it be? And what's up with that wrapped present found in the cool Cobra? Will it be easy for Dan to track down the owner? Or will it be yet *another* problem for Dan to sort out?! Find out by reading the *next* book in the series!

Want to read more
JUNKYARD DAN
books?